THE KNIGHT WHO SAID "NO!"

First published 2018 by Nosy Crow Ltd, The Crow's Nest,
14 Baden Place, Crosby Row, London SE1 1YW
www.nosycrow.com

ISBN 978 1 78800 207 3 (HB)
ISBN 978 1 78800 208 0 (PB)

Nosy Crow and associated logos are trademarks and/or
registered trademarks of Nosy Crow Ltd.

A CIP catalogue record for this book is available from the British Library.

Printed in China
Papers used by Nosy Crow are made from wood grown in
sustainable forests.

10 9 8 7 6 5 4 3 2 1 (HB)
10 9 8 7 6 5 4 3 2 1 (PB)

For my dad and Kate xx
L.R.

For Jodie
K.H.

THE KNiGHT WHO SAiD "NO!"

LUCY
ROWLAND
AND
KATE
HINDLEY

Once inside a castle lived
a little knight called Ned,
who *always* picked his toys up
and who *always* made his bed.

Ned, in all the village,
was the *one and only* child.
He was polite and kind and helpful.
He nodded and he smiled.

When asked to do the washing-up,
"YES!" is what he said.

When asked to fetch the firewood,
he would rush off to the shed.

When asked to pick the cabbages,
Ned wouldn't whine or stress.

He *always* answered *straight away*
and always answered . . .

"YES!"

And when, each night, the **dragon** came,
swooping through the sky,
the knights would holler, "Get inside!"
and, "**YES!**" Ned would reply.

This happened each and every night.
The dragon circled down
and frightened all the grown-ups
as she swept around the town.

They'd rush inside their cottages.
"Phew! That was close!" they'd say.

But Ned would watch the dragon
as she slowly flew away.

He thought he heard the dragon sigh
and give a little groan.
Ned wondered, "Is she just like me?
Perhaps she's all alone?"

But then, Ned's parents said, "Goodnight,"
and told him, "Bedtime, Ned."
And what would Ned say? . . .

"YES!" (of course)
and off he'd go to bed.

Until the morning Ned awoke
and something strange occurred.

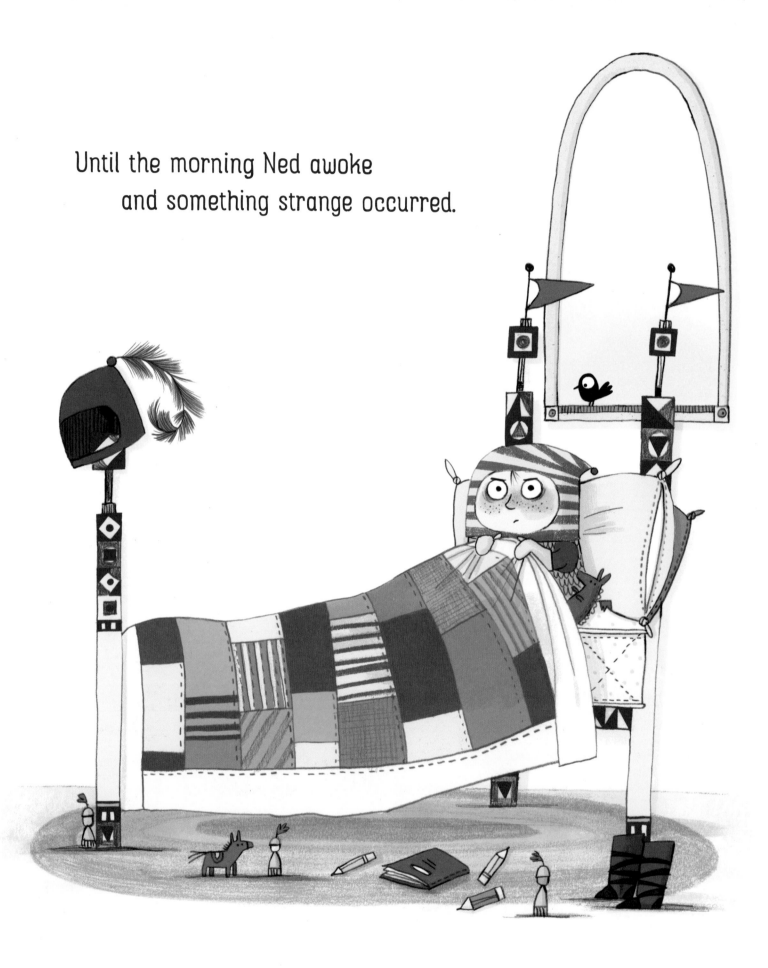

When Mum said, "Son, please fetch the milk!"
Ned found a different word.

He felt quite odd: all hot inside,
and cross from top to toe.
He shook his head from side to side
and then Ned answered . . .

"NO!"

His mum was shocked!
She stood and stared . . .

as Dad came in to say,
"Ah! Will you help me,
Ned, my lad?
The tournament's today.

Now, can you find my shield?" he asked.
"My arrow and my bow?"

But Ned still felt all prickly
and so he answered . . .

"NO!"

Well, that was just the start of it!
The "NO!"s came thick and fast!

"NO!" Ned told the butcher
when he wanted to get past.

"NO!" Ned told the baker
when she wanted Ned to pay.

"NO!" Ned told the fisherman.
"We don't want fish today!"

His parents
couldn't understand.
"What has got into Ned?"
They called him in –
"It's time for tea!" But,

"NO!"

Ned shook his head.

Suddenly, Ned heard a WHOOSH
and saw a flash of light.
The dragon, with her shiny teeth,
came soaring through the night!
The knights all shouted, "GET INSIDE!"
"Quick! Hurry, Ned!" they said.

But Ned clenched up
his fists so tight!
And...

"NO!"

yelled Ned.

The dragon circled in the sky,
then landed on the ground.
Hands on hips, Ned waited, but...
the dragon made no sound.

So Ned walked slowly up to her
and *poked* her on the toe.
"*You're* supposed to roar!" Ned said.

The dragon whispered . . .

"No . . . I'm so fed up of roaring and I'm rather lonely, too.
        I wonder," sniffed the dragon, "if there's room to stay with you?"
Ned looked quite uncertain and he nearly answered "NO!"
        But when he saw the dragon's tears, his *cross* began to go.

He didn't feel so prickly.
His *angry* was no more.
He felt a little *brighter*,
sort of *lighter*, than before.

Then Ned looked at the dragon
(trying so hard to impress)
and thought,
"There's just one thing to say."
He told the dragon . . .

The dragon loved her brand-new home!
She loved to play with Ned.

She even loved her jobs
(like fetching firewood from the shed!).

And if Ned felt bad-tempered
    (which he did, once in a while),
he'd go and find the dragon,
    who could always make him smile.

Then sometimes Ned would hear
    a shout of, "BEDTIME!" from below.
And mostly Ned would answer, "YES!"

but sometimes . . .

Ned said,
"NO!"